STARS AND STRIPES

BOOKS IN THE PUPPY PATROL SERIES ™

PUPPY PATROL ™

STARS AND STRIPES

JENNY DALE

Illustrations by Mick Reid
Cover illustration by Michael Rowe

AN
APPLE
PAPERBACK

SCHOLASTIC INC.
New York Toronto London Auckland Sydney
Mexico City New Delhi Hong Kong Buenos Aires

SPECIAL THANKS TO MARY HOOPER

No part of this publication may be reproduced in whole or in part, or stored in a retrieval system, or transmitted in any form or by any means, electronic, mechanical, photocopying, recording, or otherwise, without written permission of the publisher. For information regarding permission, write to Macmillan Publishers Ltd., 20 New Wharf Rd., London, N1 9RR Basingstoke and Oxford.

ISBN 0-439-52104-1

Text copyright © 2001 by Working Partners Limited.
Illustrations copyright © 2001 by Mick Reid.

All rights reserved. Published by Scholastic Inc., 557 Broadway, New York, NY 10012, by arrangement with Macmillan Children's Books, a division of Macmillan Publishers Ltd.

SCHOLASTIC and associated logos are trademarks and/or registered trademarks of Scholastic Inc.

12 11 10 9 8 7 6 5 4 3 2 1   3 4 5 6 7 8/0

Printed in the U.S.A.
First Scholastic printing, March 2003

CHAPTER ONE

"**W**ow!" Neil and Emily said together. Then, staring around them, they said, "Oh, wow!" again.

Neil Parker and his younger sister Emily were standing in the massive arrivals terminal at Los Angeles International Airport with their backpacks on the floor beside them. A flight attendant had helped them to get their backpacks from the luggage carousel and had told them to wait in the terminal until their friend Max arrived. Neil and Emily had just flown six hours from New York and were feeling a little lost and awestruck. This was partly because of the hugeness of the place and partly because they were a very long way from King Street Kennels, their home in the town of Compton in northwest England.

1

Neil and Emily were surrounded by people in a hurry. Everyone seemed to be pulling suitcases, running with backpacks, or marching past quickly, talking into cell phones. No one was dawdling or standing still. To eleven-year-old Neil, they all looked as if they knew exactly where they were going and wanted to get there as fast as possible.

"Where's Max, then?" Emily said in a worried voice. "He said he'd meet us here."

"Here in the arrivals terminal . . ." Neil said, looking all around him. He ran a hand through his hair, making the spiked parts stick up even more. "Trouble is, this place seems to go on for miles. I've never seen anything like it!"

Banks of TV screens above them flickered and changed, giving details of flights from everywhere in the world. Loudspeakers boomed announcements, babies yelled, and from all around came snippets of many different languages. It was overwhelming.

"He could be anywhere," Neil said, his eyes searching the crowds for Max's familiar face.

"What'll we do if he doesn't arrive?" Emily asked nervously.

"Oh, he'll show up," Neil said. "Max won't let us down."

At home in England, Max was a fairly well-known actor. He was the star of the *Time Travelers* series and had once come to Compton to make a movie, along with his dog, Prince. Neil and Emily had been chosen as extras and, during the making of the film, Neil had solved a couple of doggy problems on the set. The Parker family wasn't known as the Puppy Patrol for nothing! Since then, the three of them had been good friends. Neil and Emily had found out that Max was going to be filming in Hollywood and, as they were planning a trip to the States, they had asked their parents if they could stay with Max in Los Angeles as part of their vacation.

"We've got to call Mom, remember," ten-year-old Emily said, chewing her bottom lip. "We're supposed to let her know that we arrived safely."

Neil look at his watch and muttered to himself. "It's eight in the evening here, and eleven in New York, so it's . . . um . . . four o'clock in the morning at home," he calculated.

"She said we've got to call no matter what the time is there," Emily told him.

For a moment Neil thought of home and the boarding kennels and rescue center that their parents, Bob and Carole, ran. Traveling was exciting, but he really missed all the dogs, especially Jake, his Border collie. He missed ruffling Jake's curly hair and feeling the damp doggy nose pushed into his palm. Suddenly, Neil wanted to call home as soon as possible. "We'll call them when we get to Max's place," he said. "We haven't exactly arrived safely yet, have we? We're not quite there. Anything could happen before we actually arrive."

"Don't say things like that!" Emily laughed just as two men rushed past her, one on either side, and practically bowled her off her feet. Staggering back, she caught sight of a huge poster of Mickey Mouse with a fairy-tale castle in the background. "Look! Disneyland!" she said excitedly, forgetting for a moment that they seemed to be lost in one of the busiest airports in the world. "Do you think we will be able to go there?"

"I hope so," Neil said. "It would be crazy to come all this way and not go!"

"Won't Sarah be jealous!" Emily said.

Sarah was their five-year-old sister, who was at home with their mom and dad.

The whole family was going to meet up the following week for a short stay in Alaska, where their relatives ran a retirement home for huskies.

"She'd better not find out," Neil said. "She'll be *mad*!" Suddenly, he caught sight of Max. "There he is," he shouted. "There's Max!"

Emily gave a whoop of joy. "Max! Max!" she called.

Max gave a yell and hurried over, slapping both of his friends on the back. "Great to see you," he said. "How are you doing?"

"We're all right now that we've found you. Or you've found us," Neil said with a grin. He was pleased to see his old friend, but it seemed strange to see Max without his beloved spaniel, Prince, or

Prince's daughter, Princess, by his side. The three of them were inseparable at home.

Emily glanced around them as they walked across the marble floor. "No one's looking at you," she said, sounding rather disappointed. "I thought people would be following you around asking for autographs, like they do at home."

Max laughed. "Here in Los Angeles, *everyone's* famous! We'd better hurry," he added. "Sue-Ellen's waiting outside in her car and she's only allowed to stop for two minutes."

"Is she your guardian?" Neil asked.

Max nodded. "They call her my chaperon on the set. She's also the owner of Stripes — the doggy star."

Neil's eyes brightened immediately. "What's the dog like? I'm dying to meet him."

Max shrugged. "Oh, he's OK."

Neil glanced at him, wondering about the dull tone in his voice. It wasn't like Max to be so dismissive about a dog. He usually never stopped talking about Prince or Princess.

"Stripes is in the car with Sue-Ellen," Max added.

"Mom spoke to Sue-Ellen on the phone before we left England," Emily said. "Is she nice? Is it her house we're staying in?"

"It's her *condo*," Max corrected. "She's renting it while *Spook Spotting,* the film I'm in, is being shot."

"What's a condo?" Emily asked.

"It's what they call an apartment," Max said. "It's great — really big, with three bedrooms, and its own heated tub on the patio. And there's a big swimming pool outside in the yard."

"Awesome!" Emily and Neil said together.

The three of them emerged from the air-conditioned airport building. From where they were standing, they could see huge arching freeways crossing one another, laden with cars, and from behind them came the roar of aircraft landing and taking off. The noise and fumes were incredible and Emily edged closer to Neil.

"It's OK," Max said. "You'll get used to it. They call Los Angeles the city of the automobile." He grinned and pointed to a gleaming white stretch limousine. "Over there. Hop in!"

Neil and Emily stared and their jaws dropped in amazement.

"A stretch limo," Neil said. "Fantastic! Looks like you've really made it over here, buddy."

"Wait till we tell Mom and Dad!" Emily gasped.

But Max suddenly burst out laughing and grabbed Emily's arm to stop her from going toward the limo.

"What's up?" Emily said.

Max was speechless with laughter.

"He's putting us on!" Neil said, suddenly getting the joke. "The limo's not waiting for us at all."

"You should have seen your faces," Max said. He put his hand to his mouth in an effort to stop laughing. "Sorry," he said. "Just some L.A. humor."

"Oh, thanks a lot!" Neil said, grinning.

Emily's face fell. "I was just thinking what I'd tell my friends back in Compton."

Suddenly, there was a frantic beeping from farther along the road and a white-sleeved arm waved out the window of a parked car. "Hey, come on, you guys," came a thick American drawl. "I'll get a ticket if you don't get a move on!"

Max grabbed Emily's backpack from her and slung it over his shoulder, and the three of them ran toward the white, open-topped Jeep.

"Hi, there. I'm Sue-Ellen," the young woman sitting at the wheel said to Neil and Emily. "Welcome to Tinseltown!" Sue-Ellen had a warm smile and her bright red hair was in a ponytail on top of her head. Neil liked the look of her right away.

"This is Neil and this is Emily," Max said, throwing the backpacks onto the backseat.

Sue-Ellen nodded. "I think I could have figured that out, Max," she said, grinning. "But thank you all the same." She smiled at them and gestured to the dog sitting in a wired-off area behind the rear passenger seats. "This is the star of our film. Neil and Emily, meet Stripes."

The dog immediately sat up and looked at them. Stripes was a little smaller than Jake, Neil's Border collie, and he had big brown eyes, floppy ears, and a very appealing expression. His glossy brown-and-gold coat was striped almost as evenly as a zebra's.

Neil grinned. "You certainly suit your name. Hi, Stripes!" he said, and he put his hand through the wire to let the dog sniff it. Stripes looked at Neil as if sizing him up and gently sniffed at Neil's palm. The mutt put out a wet pink tongue and licked Neil's hand. Everyone laughed.

"Well, it looks as if Stripes approves of you," Sue-Ellen said.

"I've never seen a dog that didn't approve of Neil," Max said, getting into the passenger seat next to Sue-Ellen. Neil couldn't help noticing that Max hadn't said hello to Stripes or patted him in greeting.

Sue-Ellen turned and smiled at them all. "Get your seat belts on, kids," she said. "I'll give you a quick tour of the city and then we'll go back and have something to eat. I bet you're hungry."

"Starving!" Neil agreed as he and Emily climbed into the back. Sue-Ellen waited for a break in the cars streaming past and pulled out.

"So how was New York?" Max asked.

Neil and Emily exchanged looks. "Exciting," Neil said. He glanced behind at Stripes, who was lying down and appeared to have gone to sleep.

"At least, it was exciting for us," Emily went on. "We helped solve a mystery involving a baseball team and a dog-napping."

"Sounds interesting. Puppy Patrol to the rescue yet again!" Max said. He looked at Sue-Ellen. "That's what they call the Parker family at home — they're always in the middle of some sort of doggy adventure."

"Max has told me all about the things you get into at King Street Kennels, so let's hope you don't land in any adventures here," Sue-Ellen said with a smile.

"How's the film going?" Neil asked.

"Fine . . . great," said Sue-Ellen. She looked across at Max. "That's right, isn't it, Max?"

"Yeah, fine," Max replied. He didn't sound too sure about it, though, and Neil noticed that the edges of his mouth had turned down slightly.

"You're Stripes's trainer, then, Sue-Ellen," Emily said. "Do you have any other dogs?"

"I'm Stripes's trainer *and* owner," Sue-Ellen replied. "And I've got four other beautiful dogs back in San Francisco, where I live. My husband's looking after them while we're doing *Spook Spotting*."

"Has Stripes acted before?" Emily asked.

"Sure. He's been in two TV movies and he's a bit of a star already. This is his first big motion picture, though." Sue-Ellen looked in her rearview mirror and smiled fondly at the dog. "He's perfectly trained and he's one very smart dog."

"Four more dogs at home!" Neil said. "What kind are they? Do they all do film work? You must spend lots of time training them. Do they —"

"Whoa!" Sue-Ellen laughed. "All in good time. First, I need to get us safely onto this freeway, or motorway, as I think you call them in England."

"Sorry," said Neil, feeling slightly embarrassed. He sat back quietly, staring around him. Everything was so fast — and so huge! Even the ordinary cars seemed twice the length of the ones at home.

"Look over to your right, *now*!" Max said suddenly, and Neil's and Emily's heads shot around to see the vast white letters on a hill, which spelled out the word HOLLYWOOD.

"Wow! There it is!" Neil said. "The Hollywood sign."

"I've seen it so many times in photographs that I can't really believe I'm seeing it now," said Emily.

"Well, you sure are, honey," Sue-Ellen said. She

smiled at Emily in the rearview mirror. "I know what you feel like, though. It sends a tingle up and down my spine every time — and I've seen it hundreds of times."

"It's even better late at night," Max said. "It's lit up by four thousand lightbulbs."

The white Jeep continued into the city and turned onto Hollywood Boulevard. "This is where the stars hang out," Sue-Ellen said. "Or so they say."

Neil and Emily immediately stared through the side windows.

"First one to spot a star gets a prize," Emily said, and then she gave a shriek. "Look at that huge dinosaur! What's it doing up there?"

"Not a lot," Max said.

"That's Ripley's," Sue-Ellen explained. "It's a funny museum with all kinds of weird and wonderful stuff inside."

"Can we go?" Neil asked immediately.

"We'll try and find time," Sue-Ellen said. "But let me tell you, Hollywood is full of weird and wonderful stuff. You could spend your whole week here visiting places and still not see it all. You need to think long and hard about what you really want to do."

Emily nudged Neil. "Disneyland," she said in a low voice. "That's what I really want to do."

Neil coughed. "Will there be any time . . . I mean, do you think we can possibly go to Disneyland while we're here?"

"Been there, done that," Max said immediately.

Emily groaned.

"Yeah, but I wouldn't mind doing it again," Max said. "Do you think there'll be time, Sue-Ellen?"

Sue-Ellen glanced over her shoulder. "Not sure," she said. "I don't want to make any promises I can't keep."

Emily made a face.

"It all depends on how the filming goes," Sue-Ellen went on. "If Stripes and Max don't need to do too many retakes, we may just have a day to spare."

Neil poked Max in the back. "Hear that, buddy? You make sure you do a good job, OK?"

"OK," Max said, but once again Neil noticed that he didn't sound very enthusiastic about the filming.

What was wrong? Was it something to do with Stripes? Usually Max was almost as keen on dogs as he was. Was the doggy star acting up in some way? If so, Neil decided, he was going to do his best to make things right.

CHAPTER TWO

"Here it is!" Max said as a huge white limousine pulled into the driveway. "Here's our lift."

Neil gave his friend a nudge. "You can't fool us again that easily!"

"You must think we're really dumb," Emily added.

It was the following morning and the three friends — plus Sue-Ellen and Stripes — were outside the apartment building waiting for the car that was being sent for them from Elmwood Studios, where Max and Stripes were filming *Spook Spotting*. They'd only been there a few minutes when the enormous white limousine pulled up.

Sue-Ellen and Max just looked at each other, shrugged, and began to walk toward the limo. Stripes followed close to Sue-Ellen, casting an occasional glance back at Neil and Emily as if to ask why they weren't coming.

"Ha-ha!" Neil said. "Good joke."

Sue-Ellen opened one of the four side doors of the Cadillac and ushered in Stripes. Max gave a cheerful wave of his hand. "Aren't you coming with us?" he called, then said to Sue-Ellen, "I don't think they are. They must be going separately." He gestured across the road. "You can probably catch a bus."

The doors of the car closed behind him and Neil and Emily looked at each other uncertainly.

"Do you think it could possibly . . ." Neil began.

The big car started up and Emily suddenly dashed toward it. "Wait for us," she said. "Don't go."

The door opened again and Max peered out, a huge grin on his face. "Come on in," he said. "What are you waiting for?"

Neil caught up with Emily and they jumped in. "I can't believe we let you fool us twice!" Neil said.

Max was bent over with laughter. "Sue-Ellen arranged it last night," he said. "Just for a laugh."

"And just for today," Sue-Ellen reminded him. "Don't you guys start thinking you're Hollywood stars now!"

As the limo motored toward Elmwood Studios, in the San Fernando Valley, Max told them that all the film studios tended to be in the same area.

"Universal Studios is the biggest, of course," he

said. "You can take a four-hour tour of it. Some of the rides are amazing!"

"I suppose you've been there, as well," Emily said wistfully.

Max nodded. "I'd love to go again, though. If there's time."

"Count us in," Neil said.

As they went along, Neil and Emily craned toward the windows, trying to take in as much as possible. Stripes was lying on the backseat with them, and Neil scratched his soft head. "Stars, sights, the whole Hollywood thing — it doesn't bother you a bit, does it?" he said to the dog.

Stripes opened one eye and closed it again, and Neil smiled. This dog seemed to have a great personality. He couldn't imagine why Max hadn't really taken to him.

After traveling for about fifteen minutes on wide freeways, the car entered a wooded area and went down a winding road lined with tall trees. At the bottom there was a red-and-white barrier across the road, with a stop sign. Here the driver showed a pass to two uniformed men, the gates lifted, and the limo glided under a stone arch bearing the words ELM-WOOD STUDIOS.

Emily suddenly yelled. "Look over there! It's a real cowboy town!"

Neil leaned over to look out the window. "It's got

saloons and a blacksmith's and a sheriff's office!" he marveled. "It looks so real."

"It *is* real," Sue-Ellen told him. "Those are real buildings — not cardboard, like on some film sets." She pointed to the other side of the road. "Look over here," she said. "Across that field you can see a desert island with real palm trees."

"Oh, wow!" Neil said.

Emily's jaw dropped in amazement. "This is the most *fantastic* place!"

Ten minutes later, they were in West Five studio and actually on the set of *Spook Spotting,* which was a lighthearted fantasy. Most of the scenes took place in an old manor house, and the set consisted of a series of large rooms with dark, dusty old furniture, creaking floorboards, and cobwebby walls.

Max introduced Neil and Emily to a group of people who were standing close by.

"This is Abner," he said, indicating a lanky boy with a very short haircut and piercing blue eyes.

"Abner J. Purbeck," the boy corrected him. He looked at Emily. "You've probably seen me in *Wildlife Adventure.* It won an award."

"I . . . don't . . ." Emily stuttered, not knowing quite what to say to the first American film star she'd ever met.

"It hasn't actually been released in England yet, darling," a woman standing near him said.

"It'll get there soon, then," said Abner. "Very soon."

"This is Neil and that's Emily, my friends from back home," Max said to the woman. "This is Mrs. Purbeck, Abner's mom."

"And his agent," the woman added. She was tall and stick-thin, with bleach-blond hair and a lot of jewelry. She smiled widely at Neil and Emily, showing perfect teeth. "You can all call me Thelma." She put her arms around their shoulders. "Now, you four kids should get along just swell together. Abner is a fine mixer. He can talk to a store clerk and he can talk to the president. It's all the same to my Abner."

Neil was speechless.

"This is Mr. Harman, the director," Max said, and a small, squat man with a bald head, gold glasses, and a worried expression waved at them. "Hi, kids," he said in a distracted voice. "Sit yourselves down somewhere and keep out of trouble."

Neil and Emily exchanged glances.

"He's OK," Max said in a whisper. "His bark's worse than his bite. He's just permanently worried about going over budget."

"What does that mean?" Emily asked.

"It means they get a certain amount to spend on a film," Sue-Ellen said, "and a certain number of days in which to make it, and if it takes longer then they run out of money."

There was a bark from Stripes, who'd obviously

thought he'd been ignored long enough. Neil ruffled the dog's ears. "OK, Stripes," he said. "We know you're there."

Sue-Ellen began speaking seriously to Max. "Now," she said, "I want you to sit down with Stripes and think about the next scene you're going to do with him. Talk to him about it. I know it sounds crazy, but the more you're together and the more you communicate with each other, then the more natural you'll look when you're with him on film."

"OK," Max said. He shot a look at Neil and made a slight face.

As Sue-Ellen went to speak to Thelma, Neil frowned at Max. "What's up?" he asked.

Max shrugged and said nothing.

"I mean, I couldn't help noticing what you're like with Stripes," Neil continued. "You don't seem all that crazy about him. But he's a terrific dog."

Max sighed. "I know, and I don't know what it is — I just really miss Prince and Princess. I wish I could be filming with my own dogs instead of this . . . this *borrowed* dog."

"I know how you feel, because I miss Jake a lot, too. Why isn't Prince in this movie?" Neil asked.

"Because Stripes is a star here already. No one's heard of Prince over here," Max said glumly.

"But Stripes is really intelligent and well trained," Neil said.

"I know all that," Max said, getting up and going over to sit in a canvas chair with his name on the back. "He's not Prince, though, is he?"

Neil didn't know what to say to that.

Sue-Ellen, who hadn't heard their conversation, came over and handed Stripes a typewritten script. "Take it to Max," she said to the dog.

The dog took the sheaf of papers gently in his mouth and carried them over to Max.

"Thanks," Max said absently.

"Give him some real praise," Neil couldn't help saying. "Tell him what a smart dog he is."

Max looked up and laughed. "OK," he said. "I guess I'm going to have to watch everything I do with Stripes now that you're here." He patted Stripes and praised him, and the dog responded by sitting down, putting his head to one side, and giving a short bark.

"He's saying that's OK," Neil translated, and everyone nearby — including Mr. Harman — laughed.

"You like dogs, do you, kid?" he said to Neil.

"I *love* them!" Neil said fervently, and Mr. Harman nodded his approval.

"That's the spirit, kiddo."

At midday, after what seemed like very little actual filming, the set was cleared and everyone went off to the dining hall.

Neil and Emily went with Max. Their eyes were darting around the room. Was that Julia Roberts having coffee? Was that Leonardo DiCaprio stuffing himself with fries? No, maybe not.

"Can you see anyone famous?" Emily asked Max.

Max looked around and shook his head. "I don't think there's anyone really famous here today. Apart from me, that is," he added with a wink.

Neil gave him a push. "Listen to you!"

"There's Abner J. Purbeck," Emily said wryly. "He's famous."

Max lowered his voice. "What did you think of him?"

"Not a lot," Neil said.

"He's awful!" said Emily. "And he makes such a big deal about himself."

"I saw him in front of a mirror changing the color of his eyes with colored contact lenses," Neil said.

Max nodded. "Everyone goes on and on about the color of his beautiful blue eyes, but they're not real. He's got contact lenses in four different shades." He looked around to make sure no one was listening. "The thing is, he and his mom think he should have had the starring role in this film," he said in a low voice. "They're really annoyed that I got the big part."

"Too bad," Neil said.

"And someone else agrees with them, too," said Max.

"Who's that?" asked Neil.

"Wanda Richardson."

"Is *she* in the film?" Emily asked, impressed. "I saw her in *The Cauldron.* She played a witch."

"She plays a witch in this one, too," Max said. "In fact, she usually *is* a bit of a witch."

Emily giggled. "What's the matter with her? Is she really awful?"

"Pretty much," Max said. He looked up. "Here she is. Judge for yourself."

The director was entering the dining hall, accompanied by a tall woman wearing a bright blue cloak that swirled around her. She had white hair piled high on her head and a haughty expression. She passed their table without seeming to notice Max, but he put his hand up and waved at her. "Hello, Wanda!"

She looked down at him as if she were looking at an unpleasant insect.

"These are my two friends from home, Neil and Emily," Max continued, pretending he hadn't noticed her expression. "They're staying with me for a week or so."

Wanda gave the three a withering look. "Are they really?" she said without the slightest trace of interest in her voice. "How terribly nice for you all."

A noise that was a cross between a squeak and a growl came from a basket she carried on her arm. Neil peered in to see a small dog almost hidden under a fluffy pink blanket.

"Hey, a Chihuahua!" he said, and he put out his hand to let the dog sniff it.

Wanda jerked the basket away from him. "Do you mind?" she said. "Blossom doesn't like contact with strangers."

"But she's a Chihuahua, isn't she? They're usually good with people. They're really friendly," said Neil.

"Blossom likes my company and no one else's," Wanda said. "She's a very delicate dog."

"But they aren't usually — not the Chihuahuas I've met, anyway," Neil persisted.

"British Chihuahuas may be friendly," Wanda said, "but Blossom is American born and bred. And if I say she's delicate, then she is."

Neil shot a look at the other two, who were struggling to stop themselves from laughing. He wished he could say something cutting to Wanda, but he didn't want to cause any trouble for Max.

Wanda left them, sweeping on through the dining hall and into a small room at the side marked PRIVATE DINING. The director followed her. Neil, Emily, and Max exploded with laughter.

"What a mean woman," Neil said.

"I told you," Max hooted. "A witch on the set . . ."

". . . and a witch off!" finished Emily.

CHAPTER THREE

The following day, Neil and Emily were back at the studio, sitting inside a replica of a dining room in the manor house and watching that morning's filming. *Spook Spotting* was about a boy who had been left Blackwater Hall, a huge stately home, in the will of his rich uncle. The boy — played by Max — soon found out that the house was haunted. He had to rid the house of all its spooks and ghouls to be able to live there. Even the housekeeper, played by Wanda, turned out to be a witch in disguise.

"And wherever he goes, his trusty dog goes with him," Emily explained quietly, watching Max and Stripes creep across the set. As they moved, floorboards creaked, the wind whistled eerily, and from somewhere in the distance came the soft hooting of an owl. It all sounded — and looked — very real.

"That Stripes is one smart dog," Neil said in admiration. "He seems to pick up on every little gesture from Max."

"But sometimes Max doesn't seem to notice what Stripes is doing," Emily said in a low voice. "It's such a shame — they could make much more of things, but Max just doesn't seem to be on the same wavelength as Stripes."

Neil nodded. "I know." He shrugged. "I think Max misses Prince and Princess so much that he's thinking about them when he should be thinking about Stripes."

"It's as if he doesn't want to get too attached to Stripes because of his own dogs," Emily said thoughtfully.

On the set, Max was tapping around the wooden paneling on the walls of the dining room. Stripes was helping him, standing on his back legs and pressing the wood with his paws. When they touched a certain point, a mechanism was going to make a panel slide open, revealing a hidden room.

"Now Max is talking to Stripes without even looking at him," Neil said, starting to feel just a little impatient with his friend. "How on earth is Stripes supposed to do his best for someone who doesn't seem to care about him?"

On the set, as Max tapped exactly the right place, the paneling slid away and the secret room came into view. Wanda was standing in the middle of the room, not in her witch's costume, but disguised as the resident housekeeper of Blackwater Hall.

She looked at Max and gave a cackle. "Ha! So you've found my secret room, have you?"

The director gave a cry of annoyance. "Cut!" he shouted. "Wanda! You're supposed to be in character as a witch for this scene, not a housekeeper. Look at what you're wearing."

Wanda straightened up, waving her hand irritably. "Oh, fiddlesticks," she said. "I can't think straight at the moment. My Blossom's not well. She's hardly eaten a thing since Sunday. I just want to be back in the dressing room looking after her."

The director sighed as if he'd heard it all a thousand times before. "I wish you'd leave that ridiculous dog at home, Wanda."

She let out a shriek. "How dare you call her ridiculous! And *leave* Blossom? She *needs* me!" she exclaimed.

"OK, OK," said the director wearily. "Just get it fixed, will you? Call in a vet. Get the most expensive one you like — I'll pay."

"I've done that," Wanda snapped. "I've had the two best vets in Hollywood and they don't know a thing. Neither of them knows my Blossom like I do."

The director's eyes fell on Neil. "Well, let this boy here have a look at her, then," he said. "He certainly seems to know about dogs."

Neil stood up from his chair at the edge of the set. "You say she's not eating?" he asked Wanda politely. "What kind of food are you giving her?"

Wanda looked down her nose at him.

"Wanda . . ." the director said warningly. "We need to make some progress here. If you can't work because you're worried about your dog, then we need to do something about him."

"*Her!*" Wanda said. She gave an exasperated sigh. "I don't know why I should be telling you," she said to Neil, "but Blossom eats baby food. Jars of pureed apple or strained carrots."

Neil looked at her incredulously. He found it difficult to believe that a well-respected actress should be so ignorant about dogs that she actually fed one baby food.

"Then she's not getting enough protein," he said. "A dog needs fresh meat and something to gnaw on. She'd probably even like a bone sometimes."

"Nonsense!" Wanda said. "Her teeth should suffer dreadfully."

"That's not true —" Neil began.

"Let's take fifteen minutes," the director interrupted wearily. "Wanda, take Neil to your dressing room to look at the dog, then go to makeup and get

your witch costume on. The rest of us will take a break."

Neil followed an indignant Wanda to her dressing room, where Blossom was asleep in her basket. He picked up the tiny dog and stroked her gently, feeling Wanda's suspicious eyes on him the whole time.

"A long-haired golden Chihuahua," Neil said. "We don't have the long-haired type very much in England. And our Chihuahuas usually have black-and-tan-colored coats. She's a really great dog," he went on. Neil had seen all kinds of dogs at King Street

Kennels, in all sorts of conditions, and his first thoughts about the dog were probably right. Blossom was pretty healthy but just not getting enough meat or exercise. She was carried everywhere by Wanda in a basket, spoon-fed pureed food, and treated like a helpless baby.

When he tried to tell Wanda this, though, she hit the roof.

"I won't have you telling me how to bring up my own puppy," she said rudely.

"She's not a puppy — she's a dog," Neil pointed out. "OK, she's a small dog, but she needs fresh air and exercise like any other healthy animal."

Wanda's eyes narrowed. Neil thought that she looked just like the witch she was supposed to be playing. "I don't know who you think you are," she said, "but no scrap of a kid is going to tell *me* what to do."

Neil shrugged. He'd done what the director had asked. And if he could, he was going to help Blossom — whether Wanda liked it or not.

Filming started again twenty minutes later, but Wanda was in a foul mood and nothing seemed to go right on the set. Any scene with her in it needed to be filmed again and again. "Cut!" Mr. Harman kept roaring. "Again, from the beginning!"

An outdoor scene with just Stripes and Max in it proved difficult, too. Max was supposed to cling to the dog so that Stripes could swim with him through a moat full of muddy water, but he couldn't seem to trust the dog enough to let go of the side of the moat and act as if he were drowning.

"It's such a shame!" Thelma remarked as they stood and watched the filming. "Max doesn't seem to be able to do his stuff today. That 'boy and doggy magic' just isn't working, is it?"

Abner shook his head. "You know what they need in that part, Mom? An all-American boy." He shot a glance at Neil and Emily. "I don't know why they had to cast a Brit in the role in the first place."

"Oh, come on, Abner!" his mom said, and she turned to the others and gave them a big false smile. "You ought to let someone else have a chance. You've made it big. Let an unknown have a try."

"Max isn't unknown at home," Emily ventured.

"But he is over here, honey," Thelma said. "And it's over here that counts."

Neil and Emily were silent. Neil decided that he couldn't stand Abner J. Purbeck or Mrs. Thelma Purbeck, either.

Abner glanced up at the sky, where the sun was showing through the clouds. "I need sunblock, Mom. I don't want any freckles."

"I rubbed sunblock on you this morning, honey," Thelma said.

"I need *more* sunblock. I can feel myself turning pink," Abner insisted.

Neil looked up at the sky. "But the sun's hardly out!" he couldn't help saying.

"I've got very sensitive skin," Abner said, looking at Neil coldly. "And what would you know about the sun in California, anyway?"

Neil counted to ten, trying to keep his temper. He knew that Wanda already had it in for him; he didn't want to make another enemy.

Just then, Wanda appeared, practically breathing fire. "Blossom's jeweled collar has been stolen," she shrieked. "It's disappeared from around her neck!"

Neil spoke up. "She was wearing it earlier — when I was having a look at her," he said. "I remember loosening it a little."

"How dare you!" Wanda said. "That collar is studded with real sapphires and diamonds."

"I only loosened it because it was too tight," Neil said.

"If the kid loosened it, maybe it's fallen off," Thelma suggested.

"No! It's nowhere in the dressing room. It's been stolen!" Wanda announced dramatically. "I know it has. It's worth thousands of dollars and it's been stolen." She looked at Neil and Emily and pointed a bony finger at them. "There are only two strangers on the set — two people we don't know or trust. *You!*"

CHAPTER FOUR

"**H**ow dare she accuse us of stealing!" Emily protested again the following morning.

"No one believed her," Max said.

"Thelma did — and Abner," Emily pointed out.

"Who cares about *them*?" said Neil.

"So who did take the collar, then?" Emily asked, and the two boys just shrugged.

The three of them were walking across the courtyard of the apartments toward Sue-Ellen's Jeep to go to the studio. Stripes was with them, trotting along with his feathery tail high in the air. Suddenly, he stopped and sniffed the air. Then, to Neil's surprise, he dropped onto the pavement so that he was lying absolutely flat and still.

"Hey, look at Stripes!" Neil said. He tugged at the

leash he was holding. "Come on, boy. You've got filming to do today."

"He's playing dead," Max said, looking at the dog.

"Stripes!" Emily said. "You're not on the set now!"

Neil tugged at the leash again. But just then, as
they were all standing there staring at Stripes, they
felt a strange trembling underneath their feet.

Emily gasped. "What's happening? The ground's
shaking!"

Max knelt down and pressed his palms against
the ground. "I can feel it! It's a tremor," he said excitedly. "A little earthquake!"

The three of them stared around, a little scared,
not knowing whether to run for cover or stay where

they were. As quickly as it had started, though, the shaking stopped and everything was still again. Stripes picked himself up and began to walk off as if nothing had happened.

"Wow!" Neil exclaimed. "A real earthquake!"

"Yeah. Just a tiny one," Max said.

"Wait until I tell Mom and Dad we were in an earthquake!" Emily said, still looking stunned.

Sue-Ellen was waiting for them outside the Jeep. "Did you feel that? Exciting, eh?"

"A little too exciting," Emily said. "I didn't know you had earthquakes here."

Sue-Ellen put an arm around her shoulders. "It's nothing to be scared of, honey. Have any of you heard of the San Andreas Fault?"

They all shook their heads.

"Well, I'll explain. Basically, this area is built on what's called a fault line. It runs across two plates of land. Deep in the earth, these two plates scrape against each other, making an earthquake zone that's more than a thousand miles long, which has been shaking and moving for about sixty-five million years."

"Wow!" Neil said. "Have there been any really big earthquakes?"

"Sure," Sue-Ellen said — far too casually, Neil thought. "We had a biggie in San Francisco a few years back that wrecked our freeways. We're geared up for it in this state, though. The little tremors are no big deal and the big ones — hey, we just bear them and rebuild."

Neil was staring down at Stripes. "The funny thing is, Stripes seemed to know that tremor was coming."

Emily nodded. "He flattened himself on the ground."

Sue-Ellen opened the doors of the Jeep and ushered them in. "They say that some animals have a sixth sense about things like earthquakes, and Stripes is a real intelligent dog, you know."

Neil looked at Max. "See? He's a *very* smart dog," he said meaningfully.

Max patted Stripes rather absently. "Yeah. Sure he is." Without being told, Neil knew exactly what Max was thinking: *Prince* is a very smart dog, too.

Later that morning, Max and Abner were filming a scene in a cellar. Wanda, now in her witch costume, was in a small room off the cellar where she was supposed to be reading from a book of spells. Offstage, in Wanda's canvas chair, Blossom sat in her basket. Every now and then the little dog looked up and gave a sharp *yap-yap-yap,* driving the soundman crazy.

With each *yap,* Mr. Harman got more and more irritated.

"Wanda," he said finally, "is it at all possible for you to leave that dog of yours in the dressing room?"

"My dressing room isn't safe," Wanda replied crossly. "Blossom's jeweled collar was stolen. If I leave Blossom there, she might get stolen, too."

"If that happened, we might all get a little peace," the director said under his breath. He snapped his fingers. "Hey, kid," he called to Neil. "Could you take Blossom for a walk off the set, please?"

"Walk?" Wanda shrieked. "Blossom doesn't walk. She gets driven."

"Not today she doesn't," the director said. "Besides, all dogs like walks, even I know that. Dogs and walks — they go together."

Neil stood up, eager to spend some time with the little Chihuahua. He'd actually brought a small piece of steak for her — very small, because he knew better than to change Blossom's diet too suddenly — and he wanted to see if she'd eat it. He was sure that a bad diet was one of the reasons she was so sluggish.

The director thrust Blossom's basket at him and, amid shrieks from Wanda not to let her "darling dawgie's" paws touch the dirty floor, Neil carried her off, smiling to himself.

Just outside the studio in which they were filming, there was a plot of grass where Stripes was usually taken for his exercise. Neil carefully set Blossom down there and encouraged her to move.

At first, the tiny dog looked bewildered, sniffing the grass and looking around as if she were in a to-

tally alien landscape. Neil walked a few paces away
and, after a moment, Blossom followed rather un-
steadily. Neil continued walking slowly, encouraging
the Chihuahua to follow.

After a few moments of this, Neil took the little
piece of steak, which he'd wrapped in a paper nap-
kin, out of his pocket and put it down in front of
Blossom. She ate it as if she'd never seen a decent
piece of meat before in her life. *Which might well be
true,* Neil thought.

After a little more exercise, Neil decided to stop.
He knew he shouldn't tire her too much — not when
it looked as if she'd never had any regular exercise
before. He carried her back to Wanda's dressing

room and settled her into her basket, then went back to the set, reporting to Wanda that Blossom seemed absolutely fine now. Wanda merely gave him a withering look and turned her back.

Neil told Emily in a whisper how he'd made out, then they settled down to watch the next part of filming. This was still set in the cellar, where Abner was supposed to be tied up with invisible ropes. The scene required Max and Stripes to find him and set him free.

"Something funny's going on," Emily whispered to Neil. "When Abner gets free of the ropes, he has to stretch his arms and punch the air because he's so pleased about it. Each time he does, though, he seems to punch Max. You watch."

"Quiet, please. Scene fourteen, take six," a man called, snapping the black-and-white clapper board in front of the camera.

Neil watched as Stripes and Max went through their actions and the invisible ropes were removed. Abner stretched out, flailed his arms around — and socked Max hard on the upper arm.

"Hey!" Max shouted. "You don't have to do that every time, do you?"

Abner looked surprised. "Did I get you by accident?" he asked innocently.

Standing beside Max, Stripes gave a soft growl. Neil had already noticed that Stripes seemed to stick up for Max whether they were acting or not.

"You've managed to 'get me by accident' each time," Max said.

Abner gave a completely false smile. "Oh. So sorry!"

Mr. Harman stood up and walked over to the two boys. "What is it between you guys?" he said. "You're supposed to be buddies, right? You're not supposed to be arguing."

"We're just joking, Mr. Harman," Abner said, and he gave Max a playful punch on the same arm. "Right, pal?"

"Right," Max muttered, rubbing his arm as he walked back to the side of the set.

Thelma, who'd been standing to one side and watching anxiously, came forward to stand by Mr. Harman. "It's such a shame," Neil heard her say. "These scenes just don't seem to be working, do they?"

Mr. Harman shrugged. "We'll get there."

"It would be nice if Abner could have a slightly bigger part. He's got such a following with the girls, you know! You should see his fan mail."

"Yeah. You've told me about it before," the director said. "Any slightly bigger part would involve working with Stripes, though, and your son doesn't really like dogs, does he?"

"Not like dogs?" Thelma's voice rose incredulously. "My boy dotes on dogs. He loves Stripes! Adores him!"

The director shook his head wearily. "OK, OK. Tell me later, Thelma." He called over to his assistant. "Let's have another take, please."

The man with the clapper board came forward. "Quiet, please. Scene fourteen, take seven!"

Eventually, after three more takes, the director called, "It's a wrap!" That meant the scene had been shot to his satisfaction and so could be finished, or wrapped up. Neil noticed that Abner had managed to get in a couple more sly punches during that time.

A break was called and Max came over to Neil and Emily, saying he was starving. The three of them were just about to go to the dining hall with Stripes and Sue-Ellen when Wanda came steaming onto the set.

"Stop, thief!" she cried.

They all looked at one another.

"What do you mean by that, Wanda?" Mr. Harman sighed.

"Blossom's bowl is missing! Her gold bowl has disappeared from my dressing room!"

"Who'd ever want to steal a dog bowl?" Mr. Harman asked, exasperated.

"That bowl is worth a great deal of money," Wanda said. "It was handmade by a goldsmith to the queen of England." She raised her hands to her head dramatically. "I just can't take much more of this! Blossom is desperately ill, her favorite things are being stolen — it's all quite intolerable. I've never known so much trouble on a film before." She pointed at Neil and Max. "It must be one of those boys. Boys are always up to no good."

To Neil's surprise, Thelma stepped forward. "Now, come on, Wanda," she said. "You're being a little hasty here."

"That boy" — Wanda pointed to Neil — "has been in my dressing room on his own."

"I only went to put Blossom back!" Neil said. "I was in there less than a minute."

"It doesn't take but a minute to steal a dog bowl," Wanda said coldly.

Thelma smiled toothily. "You mustn't be too quick in your accusations, Wanda," she said. "Any one of us could have slipped back there unseen and taken the gold bowl." She looked around the set at random and her eyes fell on Max. "Max, for instance. He disappeared just before the scene in the cellar started."

"I went to get a Coke from the machine!" Max protested.

"Of course you did," Thelma said smoothly. "That's just what I'm saying. Any one of us could have gone off unseen."

Emily's face was red with indignation. "Neither Max nor Neil would steal anything!"

"I second that," Sue-Ellen said.

"No, no, of course they wouldn't steal anything," Thelma said hurriedly. "Perish the thought. I just wanted to make the point that any one of us could have taken that bowl and collar. It didn't have to be a Brit. The fact that it *seems* to be is —"

Mr. Harman clapped his hands. "That's enough!" he said. "I don't know what's going on here, but these incidents with kids and dogs and dog bowls are seriously affecting filming. We need to get it together bigtime if we're not going to go over budget. I'm sure the bowl will turn up somewhere, and if it doesn't, we'll call the cops. In the meantime, let's have some lunch and then get back here and really get down to it!"

After lunch, Neil and Emily watched and listened as Sue-Ellen chatted with Max and Stripes.

"OK, this is your big scene, boys," she said to boy and dog. Max was sitting on his canvas chair with Stripes obediently at his feet, and both were listening to Sue-Ellen intently. "Remember, Max, this is where you're tied up in a barn, and Stripes bites away the rope to free you just before the whole place goes up in flames."

Max nodded, looking a bit worried.

"And you don't have to look like that — the fire gets filmed elsewhere. Mr. Harman wouldn't take any risks with you," Sue-Ellen assured him.

"I wasn't worried about that," Max said.

"I want you to sit down with Stripes and go through this scene with him like you did before," Sue-Ellen said. "I want you to talk to him — really talk. I want to see some understanding between the two of you. I want *magic!*"

As Max nodded, Neil tapped Emily on the arm. "Let's go off and leave him alone," he whispered. "It might be easier for him if we're not here."

"Where should we go?" Emily asked. "Back to the dining hall?"

Neil shook his head. "I've got a better idea. Those stolen things have to be somewhere, right?"

Emily nodded.

"So let's try to find them. Let's solve the mystery."

"Great idea!" said Emily.

CHAPTER FIVE

"**W**here should we start?" Neil asked. "Those things could be anywhere."

Emily bit her lip. "Now, let's think. Who would take things like that? They're obviously really valuable, so is it someone who's broke? Someone who's going to sell them and get the money?"

"Maybe," Neil said, looking baffled. "But everyone around here seems to have plenty of money. Maybe it's someone who just wants to make trouble on the set."

They began by trying to look around the West Five wardrobe department, but were chased off by a very haughty woman who was dressed exotically in a long green dress and matching turban.

"It's just as well," Neil said. "We wouldn't have known where to start in there."

"Rows and rows and *rows* of clothes," Emily said in awe as the door was firmly closed behind them.

"Let's begin hunting a little closer to home," Neil said. "I think we should start with everyone's dressing rooms." He held up a long thin key. Since the things were missing from Wanda's room, Mr. Harman had insisted that all the dressing rooms be locked while filming was going on. "Max gave me the master key earlier. This opens his room — and everyone else's on the set."

Emily gasped. "We shouldn't!"

"We'll have to," Neil said, trying to sound confident. "And then we can eliminate every single person on the *Spook Spotting* set, can't we?"

Emily's eyes widened. "We'll get killed if we're caught!"

"Then we won't get caught," Neil said. He frowned. "People will only find out we've been in them if we actually find something."

The dressing rooms of the cast of *Spook Spotting* were some distance from the set where filming was taking place. Abner's, Wanda's, and Max's rooms were in a row, and opposite them were some smaller dressing rooms for the minor characters in the film.

Neil and Emily went into Abner's room first. It was simply furnished with a table, bookshelf, and a couple of easy chairs. There weren't many places you could have hidden a gold dog bowl and jeweled collar. The one thing it didn't lack, though, was photographs of Abner: Abner in historical costume, Abner in casual clothes, Abner in sporting gear; Abner laughing, crying, astonished, wistful, and moody, all over the walls.

"Abner . . . Abner . . . Abner . . ." Emily said, looking around.

"In every film he's ever been in," Neil said. "Big-headed or what?"

"No wonder he hates playing second fiddle to Max," Emily remarked.

"It'll do him good," Neil said wryly.

The two of them searched the room swiftly and went out. "No gold bowl," Emily said. "Too bad. I wish we *had* found it hidden in there."

Wanda's dressing room was next. As they went in, Blossom, who was in her basket, lifted her head and recognized Neil at once. She gave a little yelp of greeting. As usual, like almost every dog he came into contact with, Blossom responded to Neil and seemed to trust him instinctively.

"Hello, Blossom!" Neil said, going over to pet the dog. She sat up in her basket, her eyes big in her tiny golden face, and looked up at him hopefully. Neil thought she'd probably begun to associate him with real food.

"She's really cute," Emily said.

"'Course she is." Neil felt in his pocket for a dog

biscuit, found one, and gave it to Blossom. The little dog started to gnaw at it with obvious delight. "It's only the old witch who's made her into such a wimp."

"Well, I hope she's finished that biscuit by the time the old witch comes back or she'll know you've been in here," Emily warned.

"You wait. Blossom'll have that down in about thirty seconds flat."

"Do we really have to look around in here?" Emily asked. "It's not likely that Wanda would steal her own stuff, is it?"

Neil shrugged. "She might have misplaced the things. She's pretty scatterbrained, isn't she? Maybe she's just forgetful."

They made a quick search, but apart from noticing that Blossom now had a new *silver* drinking bowl and matching collar, they found nothing of interest.

Max's dressing room was next.

"We might as well have a quick look," Neil said. "Then when we're done, we'll know that we've examined every single cast member's dressing room."

"And we know we won't find anything in here, don't we?" Emily said. As she spoke, she lifted a cushion on an easy chair, then gave a little scream. *"Oh, no!"*

Neil wheeled around. There, under the cushion, were the jewel-encrusted collar and the gold bowl. He gave a gasp of horror.

"Here in Max's room!" Emily said. "Oh, no." She

stared at Neil and he stared back at her, incredulous. "What should we do?"

"I don't know . . . I . . ."

Just as he was speaking, the door to the dressing room was pushed open farther and Wanda stood there. She gave a high-pitched scream. "My things! Blossom's treasures!"

"We just . . . just . . ." Emily stuttered.

"Look, we don't know how they got here," Neil said quickly, "but it's obviously some sort of misunderstanding. . . ."

Wanda snatched up the bowl and collar, then went to the door. "Help! Call the cops!" she shouted.

Neil and Emily looked at each other despairingly. Both of them knew there was no stopping Wanda now.

Thelma was first on the scene, quickly followed by Abner, then Max with Sue-Ellen and Mr. Harman.

"What on earth's going on now?" Mr. Harman demanded.

"My Blossom's things have been found," Wanda announced, holding the bowl and collar high. "Discovered in the dressing room of" — she paused theatrically and pointed at Max — "*that boy!*"

"What do you mean?" Max said indignantly. "How did you find them in here? I didn't take them. I haven't seen them since they disappeared."

"Then what were they doing hidden here?" Wanda said. She looked at Max through narrowed eyes. "And it wasn't anything to do with *me*. Your so-called friends were the ones who found them."

Max looked at Neil, puzzled. "You found them? What were you looking in here for?"

"Sorry, Max," Neil said, feeling awful. "We were searching everywhere for the missing things, in all the dressing rooms, and we thought we'd better look in here as well, and . . ."

"They were under the cushion, but we don't think for one minute you took them," Emily said. She gestured around at the others. "No one does."

Mr. Harman and some of the others murmured agreement, but they were obviously annoyed that Neil and Emily had been in their dressing rooms. There was a conspicuous silence from Abner and Wanda. In fact, Neil noticed that Abner was trying to hide the smirk on his face.

"Of course Max didn't take them!" Thelma cried.

"As if a nice English boy would steal our possessions." She crossed to Max and put her arms around him. "The poor kid's far away from home — and maybe he doesn't understand about American laws and things. After all, look at the way his friends thought they could just go into our dressing rooms," she finished smugly.

Neil and Emily looked at each other again. Thelma was making things worse!

"Max isn't a thief," Emily burst out.

Neil heard a low whine and saw Stripes leave Sue-Ellen's side and push himself through several sets of legs to find Max. The dog stood by Max, looking up at him loyally, as if to say that *he* believed in him.

"Look, Max did *not* take those things!" Neil said in frustration. "I'd bet a million dollars on it."

Mr. Harman grinned at him. "That won't be necessary, young man," he said. He turned to the rest of the film crew. "Now, I don't know what's been happening, but if this is someone's idea of a joke, it's not funny. I refuse to let it disrupt filming, however. Wanda, your dog has her trinkets back, and I suggest she look after them a little better in the future. Neil and Emily, you stay out of people's dressing rooms. No harm has been done, and I want everyone back on the set in two minutes."

Sue-Ellen gave Max a reassuring hug and then she and everyone else left the dressing room. Neil and Emily hung back to talk to their friend.

"Sorry, Max," Neil said again. "We didn't mean to get you in trouble."

Max shrugged. "That's OK." He glanced at Neil and added in a low voice, "I don't know what's happening on this film, though. I just don't feel right about anything."

"What do you mean?" Neil asked.

"I hate all the tension on the set, and I don't trust Abner," said Max. "I can't help feeling that he's really got it in for me."

"There's not much he can do," Neil said, trying to reassure him. "Emily and I will keep an eye on him."

"And his mom, Thelma. I don't like her much, either," Max went on gloomily.

"I think Wanda's worse," Neil said. "I think she's the one you've got to watch out for."

Back on the set ten minutes later, Mr. Harman was studying his clipboard. "OK. We're going to do the scene following the moat rescue. You, kid" — he gestured to Max — "will need to get sprayed with water, because Stripes has just helped you get out."

"This is where I come in with the magic cloak of invisibility!" Abner put in excitedly. "Max and I discuss what's gone on, and then I throw the cloak over him and the dog, and they both disappear. After that, we go off into the manor house." He looked at Thelma. "I get to change character when we reach the manor. I change from Mr. Nice Guy to a wicked villain."

"You do, darling," Thelma said. "And you do it so convincingly."

But Mr. Harman was waving his script. "Sorry, folks, I've had to make some changes here."

Abner frowned. "Not to *my* part."

"Afraid so," Mr. Harman said as Neil and Emily exchanged secret, gleeful glances. "Having looked again at the complete script, I don't see that it's necessary for you to be in this moat scene at all. It holds up the action too much. What I want now is for Stripes to discover the cloak, and for him to carry it to Max in his teeth. We'll get some real funny shots of the dog being half invisible. Parts of him will keep appearing and disappearing as he runs."

"Good idea!" Sue-Ellen said enthusiastically.

"But that's my big scene!" Abner protested. He turned to Thelma. "It's my big one, Mom!"

"I know, honey." Thelma turned to Mr. Harman. "Some of my kid's best lines are in that scene. He was going to be amazing!"

"I'm sure he was," Mr. Harman said dryly, "but now he'll just have to be amazing in the other scenes instead."

Abner suddenly threw his script on the floor. "It's not fair!" he whined.

"No, it isn't," Wanda said, stepping forward. "The kid is a good actor. He ought to have a much bigger part in this film. He ought to be the star."

"The star of this film is a dog," Mr. Harman

pointed out calmly. "Stripes is the real star, and I don't think we ought to lose sight of that."

Stripes, who was sitting beside Neil, pricked up his ears on hearing his name. Neil ruffled his fur. "That's you they're talking about," he whispered. "You're the big name here."

Stripes pushed his nose against Neil's hand and licked him, as if to say thank you.

"You know what I mean," Wanda continued impatiently. "Abner ought to have the lead human role."

"Maybe he should, but on this occasion he doesn't," the director replied crisply.

There was a moment's silence, then Abner turned on his heel. "This is just stupid. *Stupid!*" he said, and he gave Max a venomous look and strode off the set.

Thelma ran after him. "Sorry, everyone!" she trilled. "Artistic temperament, you know."

Max shot a look at Neil and Emily and the three of them tried to grin reassuringly at one another. Stripes gave a growl and Neil thought he knew exactly what it meant. Stripes didn't seem to trust Abner and his mother any more than they did.

CHAPTER SIX

"That was incredible!" Neil said. "I want to go on everything all over again, especially the Jurassic Park ride."

"You'll get sick," Emily said. She frowned. "Besides, I thought the Waterworld ride was the best."

"You're both crazy," Max said. "The Back to the Future ride was the best by miles!"

Neil, Emily, and Max had just come back from spending a whole afternoon at Universal Studios and were sitting in the yard that surrounded Sue-Ellen's apartment building. They were stretched out on lounge chairs, catching the last rays of the sun as it set over Beverly Hills.

It was the day following the discovery of the stolen items on set, and filming had finished early, partly because it was Sunday, and partly because everyone needed a break. Neil, Emily, and Max had pleaded with Sue-Ellen to take them to Disneyland, but she insisted that it wasn't worth going for half a day. She'd suggested that they save Disneyland for the end of their stay. If all went well with *Spook Spotting,* Max would have a whole day off before Neil and Emily had to leave.

The good-natured arguing about the merits of the various Universal Studios rides went on until Emily got fed up. "Oh, stop it, you two," she said, putting up her hands. "They were all great. All fantastic. All *equal.*"

The two boys frowned but decided to let Emily have the last word. Neil put out his hand to ruffle Stripes's golden ears. The mutt was stretched out on the grass between him and Max. "Yeah, well, whatever ride was best, you would have loved it there, Stripes. It was completely exciting," he sighed.

"I think Stripes would have been completely confused," Sue-Ellen said, coming out with a tray of iced drinks. "I don't think he'd have enjoyed going on those roller coasters at all!"

Suddenly, Stripes lifted his head, sniffed the air, and flattened himself to the ground with his eyes closed.

"Hey, is this another tremor?" Neil asked, watching the dog closely.

As Sue-Ellen put the tray of drinks down, Neil felt

the ground move very slightly beneath them. The ice in the glasses shivered and clinked.

"I believe it was," Sue-Ellen said. "I barely felt it, though."

"Stripes did," Neil said. "*And* he knew it was coming." He fished an ice cube out of his drink and gave it to the dog to crunch. "Good boy, Stripes! Smart boy!" As Neil spoke, he shot a look at Max, frustrated that *he* didn't praise the dog and make a fuss over him as well.

Things still weren't right between Max and Stripes — Neil knew that. In the important scene the day before, when Stripes had found the cloak of invisibility, the action with Stripes on his own had gone well. The dog was fantastically well trained and quick, seeming to know instinctively what was expected of him. As soon as Max was acting with him, however, their performances appeared stilted and lifeless. Mr. Harman had called for one take after another and didn't seem satisfied with the end result at all.

"I wonder when I'll see Prince and Princess again," Max suddenly said longingly.

"If the filming goes on schedule, in another ten days," Sue-Ellen said. She made a face, adding, "And if it doesn't go on schedule, who knows?" She looked at Neil and Emily. "Now, you two fly to Alaska next Thursday, don't you?"

Emily nodded. "We're going to stay at my aunt and uncle's place."

"They take in old huskies who can't work anymore," Neil explained.

"It sounds like you have Puppy Patrol centers all across the globe," Sue-Ellen said.

"Almost!" Neil replied with a grin. He looked at Sue-Ellen hopefully. "Do you think we might get to Disneyland before Thursday?"

"Maybe," Sue-Ellen said. "No promises, though."

"But anyway, Universal Studios was fantastic," Emily said, not wanting to sound ungrateful.

Sue-Ellen looked at the three of them. "Now," she said, "when you've finished those drinks, I want you all to put on your best outfits."

"Are we going out?" Emily asked excitedly.

"We sure are," Sue-Ellen said. "Our little gang is going to hit Hollywood!"

"I don't believe it," Neil said, his jaw gaping. "I just don't believe it."

"What don't you believe?" Emily asked, hanging out the window of the Jeep and taking one last look at the house that Sue-Ellen said had once belonged to Macaulay Culkin.

"I just saw a dog — a full-sized poodle and . . ." Neil's voice trailed away.

"And what?" Max prompted.

"It was a light-haired dog — white, I guess — but its fur was dyed *pink*. And it was wearing a suit. A white jacket with little pants!" Neil suddenly exploded with laughter. "White pants! Short white pants!"

"Not *really*?" Emily said.

"Honest." Neil shook his head wonderingly. "OK, it's funny, but it's not very nice for the dog, is it? You'd probably get arrested for dressing your dog up like that at home."

"I don't know whether I believe you," Emily said, craning her head around to see if she could catch a glimpse of the pink pet.

Sue-Ellen looked at Emily in her rearview mirror. "You'd better believe it," she said. "I've seen the same thing. I've seen a dog wearing a diaper here — and one wearing a bikini."

"No!" Neil said. "That's crazy." He looked over his shoulder at Stripes, who was sitting patiently behind the wire grill. Neil couldn't imagine anyone wanting to cover up Stripes's beautiful brown-and-gold coat with ridiculous clothes.

"It shouldn't be allowed. Mom and Dad wouldn't believe this place," said Emily.

"Do you get people dressing up their dogs like that in San Francisco, where you come from?" Max asked.

Sue-Ellen shook her head. "No way. We're slightly crazy in San Fran — but not *that* crazy."

"Look at that!" Emily suddenly yelled. "We just passed a great big pile of records."

"I missed it," Neil said. "I was looking for more dressed-up dogs. What was it?"

"The Capitol Records building," Max said, grinning. "It's wonderful, isn't it? It's shaped like a huge stack of records."

Sue-Ellen drove on down Rodeo Drive, which was lined with expensive shops, and onto Hollywood Boulevard. She parked and everyone piled out, Neil holding Stripes on a leash.

"First of all, we're going to Mann's Chinese Theatre," Sue-Ellen said. "No visit to Hollywood is complete without going there."

"What's that?" Emily asked.

"It's the place where all the big film stars have put their hands and feet in the cement," Max explained. Neil knew at once what he meant.

With Sue-Ellen leading the way, they walked down to the theater, gazing in awe at the luxurious shops. There were tons of tourists everywhere, taking photographs of their favorite stars' hand- and footprints, which had been preserved forever in cement.

Neil walked slowly along with Stripes beside him, studying each white square carefully until he came to the one he was looking for. "At last," he said. "Lassie! Here are her paw prints."

"Who's Lassie?" Emily asked.

"A famous dog. A *very* famous dog who starred in lots of films," Neil said.

"I think she's the only dog here," Sue-Ellen said. "And the only other four-legged creature is a horse named Champion."

Neil bent down to feel the concrete paw prints. "Have a try," he said, bringing Stripes closer. "Let's see if your paws fit into Lassie's."

Stripes's paws were a little smaller than Lassie's. "Hey! Couldn't we get Stripes's paw prints here?" Neil asked. "He's almost as famous."

"Not *quite* as famous as Lassie," Sue-Ellen said, shaking her head. "Maybe he will be one day, though." She smiled. "Maybe when *Spook Spotting* is released."

"If Stripes *does* get to make paw marks in the cement here, I want to come back and see it," Emily said.

"It's a deal," Sue-Ellen said. "Now, I don't know about the rest of you, but I'm absolutely starving. Let's go eat."

They couldn't go anywhere really fancy because they had Stripes with them, but Sue-Ellen managed to get them a table outside one of the big theme restaurants just off Hollywood Boulevard. This one was decorated in Mexican style, with false tiled house fronts, big green cactus plants, and sand strewn on the floor. They sat at a round table under a palm tree, with an incredibly real-looking waxwork Mexican man beside them.

It took them fifteen minutes just to read through

the menu, and even then no one could make up their mind about what to have.

"Everything sounds wonderful. I can't decide between the chicken gumbo or the shrimp jambalaya," said Emily.

"I'm going to have the Cajun beef," Max said. "Or I might have the seafood enchilada."

"It says here that their hamburgers are award-winning and the best in the world," Neil said, his tongue almost hanging out. "But would I be able to eat one if I had the cowboy's breakfast hot 'n' spicy largest ribs in the world first?"

"Well, if you want to eat anything tonight, you'd better decide soon," Sue-Ellen said, laughing.

The waiter came up and grinned at them. "Do you want to hear today's specials?" he asked. "We've got fresh barbequed salmon to start and a Mexican chili to die for."

Everyone groaned.

"Can you give us another five minutes to choose?" Sue-Ellen said.

When the food started arriving, Stripes sat quietly until Neil's award-winning hamburger came to the table. As Neil was about to dig in, he heard the dog give a few plaintive whines as a golden-brown nose appeared from under the tablecloth.

"I've got something saved for you," Neil said, and he picked up a meaty rib bone from the edge of his

plate. "It's one of the hot 'n' spicy largest ribs in the world." He looked at Max. "Why don't you give it to Stripes?" he asked. "He'll love it."

Max shook his head. He had been a little quiet all evening and Neil thought that maybe he was missing Prince and Princess again. "Oh, go on," Neil urged him. He really wanted to help Max bond with Stripes.

Max popped a few fries into his mouth. "That's OK," he said. "You give it to him."

Neil shrugged, then waved the rib. "Here you go, then, Stripes," he said, lifting the red tablecloth. "Remember your under-the-table manners."

Neil passed Stripes the bone and the dog took it eagerly. There was a short bark swiftly followed by a crunch, and everyone laughed.

Max sighed. "Can I call home when we get back to the apartment?" he asked. "I want my mom to get Prince and Princess to bark on the phone to me."

Neil looked at him and raised his eyebrows. So much for bonding with Stripes. . . .

"Sure you can," Sue-Ellen said. "And then it's straight to bed for all of us. You and I, Max, have an early call at the studio tomorrow. We've got to be there by seven o'clock."

"How will Neil and I get there?" Emily asked.

"Don't worry," Sue-Ellen said. "I'll send a car back for you."

"A stretch limo?" Emily suggested hopefully.

"Not a stretch limo!" Sue-Ellen laughed. "That was a one-time-only event."

On the way home, Emily leaned against Neil, yawning. "Didn't we have a fantastic day?" she sighed.

"Totally," Neil agreed.

She lowered her voice. "Do you think we'll get to Disneyland?"

"Don't know," Neil said. "I hope so." But judging by the way the filming was going — with all the retakes and the mysterious thefts — he was beginning to feel doubtful.

CHAPTER SEVEN

"**I** love it here," Emily said the next morning, her nose pressed against the window of the car that was taking them to the studio. "There are just so many things happening all the time. I'd like to live here forever, wouldn't you?"

"Yeah, but . . ." Neil thought about King Street Kennels. He thought about waking up in the crisp early morning and taking a group of dogs on a walk across the fields before school. And then he thought of Jake. "Nah," he said firmly. "It's great here, but home's best."

As they passed one of the many drive-through eating places just outside Los Angeles, Emily said happily, "We'll be just in time for brunch in the studio dining hall."

"I'm having eggs over easy," Neil said right away.

"What's that?" asked Emily.

"It means they flip fried eggs over and then take them straight out of the pan."

"I'm having a spinach omelette with maple syrup," Emily said.

Neil made a face. "Yuck!"

"I saw someone having maple syrup on their ham and eggs yesterday," Emily told him.

"That's disgusting!" Neil said.

"I don't care," said Emily. "I want to try it."

The driver had been instructed to take Neil and Emily to the West Five studio, where shooting was still going on inside the dining room of the haunted manor house. As they walked through the piled-up scenery and came into view of the set, Neil noticed that there was a little group of people clustered around Mr. Harman.

When the director saw Neil, he gave a shout. "Here's his pal! Is he with you, Neil?"

"Who? Do you mean Stripes?" Neil asked, bewildered. Then he noticed that Sue-Ellen, who was looking worried, had Stripes on a leash by her side.

"No, I mean *Max*. We're looking for Max," Mr. Harman said.

Neil shook his head, confused.

"We haven't seen Max at all," Emily said. "He left first thing this morning with Sue-Ellen."

Sue-Ellen nodded. "We got here before seven and Max said he was hungry and went off to have some breakfast in the dining hall. I got coffee from the machine and went to his dressing room to wait for him. I waited and waited but he never arrived. I even called the apartment after you two left in case he'd gone back there, but there was no answer."

"Should I go and search in the dining hall?" Neil asked.

"We've done that," Mr. Harman said. "And we've looked in all the dressing rooms in the block. There's just no sign of him." He looked at Neil hard. "Was Max worried about anything? Did he say anything to you?"

Neil shrugged. "No. Nothing at all."

"He was a little quiet this morning," Sue-Ellen volunteered. "I just thought he was tired, though."

"He's been worried about Prince and Princess — his dogs at home," Emily said.

"Hey, you don't think the crazy kid's run off home to England to see his dogs, do you?" Thelma asked suddenly.

"No, I'm sure he hasn't," said Sue-Ellen. "Max is a responsible actor. He wouldn't do something like that."

"That's what *you* say," put in Wanda maliciously. "It seems to me he's done nothing but cause trouble on this set. And I still believe he took —"

"For goodness' sake, Wanda," Mr. Harman interrupted her. "It will do no good at all to bring that up again."

Sue-Ellen went over and spoke in a low voice to Mr. Harman. "Look, I'm responsible for Max's welfare while he's working on this film, so if he's missing it's up to me to find him."

Neil felt very confused. What on earth was Max up to — going off like that and worrying everyone?

Mr. Harman put an arm around Sue-Ellen's shoulders. "Come on, now," he said. "Maybe it won't be too bad. Maybe he's taken a couple of hours off to sort out the next big scene in his head. Let's not get too worried about him yet."

"I'm sure he hasn't gone off anywhere — off the set, I mean," Neil said. "He's as eager to get this film finished as everyone else."

"Not as eager as I am," Mr. Harman said dryly. He clapped his hands. "OK, folks. We'll presume that Max has gone off for a while to get his head together, and while we wait for him we'll shoot some footage that doesn't need him."

Abner had been quiet all this time, but now he suddenly perked up. "Maybe I could take over Max's part, Mr. Harman, sir," he said. "I could be his stand-in." As everyone looked at him, he added, "Just until Max turns up, of course."

Neil and Emily exchanged indignant glances. "Talk about jumping in with both feet," Neil whispered.

"What a good idea, Abner," Wanda said. "Let's try a little homegrown talent here."

Mr. Harman looked at Abner thoughtfully. "Maybe it might be useful to have you do that, Abner. Just until Max turns up, though."

Thelma prodded Abner in the back. "Go get your script quickly, son," Neil heard her whisper. "Show Mr. Harman what you can do."

"I already know Max's part by heart," Abner said smugly.

As Thelma flashed her teeth in a smile, Neil and Emily fumed with annoyance.

"He's got such a memory, my boy," Thelma said. "He only has to look at a sentence to memorize it."

Neil nudged Sue-Ellen. *Say something!* he urged her silently. He could see that if Abner got to stand in for Max, then he could end up taking over completely. Max might find himself out of a job.

"I agree it might be helpful for Abner to step in until Max turns up," Sue-Ellen said. "But there's one big snag — Abner and Stripes don't really hit it off together, do they?"

"Don't hit it off together?" Abner repeated, his famous blue eyes widening. "Sure we do." He took a cellophane packet out of his pocket and rustled it. "Come on, boy!" he called to Stripes. "Doggy treats! Over here."

Neil watched and willed Stripes not to go to him. But it looked as if the lure of a treat was going to

be too great. Stripe's ears had pricked up at the rustling of the bag and his nose was twitching. He took one . . . two . . . three steps toward Abner, stood still for a moment, and then, to Neil's immense relief, began to back off, looking straight at Abner all the time.

Neil smiled to himself. Good old Stripes wasn't fooled! He wasn't going to be bought that easily.

"Guess he's not hungry!" Abner said, trying to make light of it. Neil could tell by the tone of his voice, though, that he was pretty annoyed.

"Well, let's see what happens when we're shooting," Mr. Harman said. "Wanda, I'll need you as a witch."

"No change there, then," Neil said to Emily under his breath, and Emily giggled.

Sue-Ellen, looking pale and worried, handed Stripes's leash to Neil.

"Take care of him for a while, will you? I'm going to the dining hall to have some coffee and think." She looked at Neil intently. "Are you sure you don't have any idea where Max is? Did he say anything to you?"

"About what?" asked Neil.

"About anything. I know he's worried about the film. I know he hasn't really taken to Stripes — not the way that he should have." As Neil began to protest, she added, "No, Neil, I can tell. The link between boy and dog should be like a strong, invisible rope, binding them together. Stripes and Max just don't have that rope."

Neil bit his lip, not knowing what to say. As Sue-Ellen went off, Emily clutched his arm. "Where do you think Max has gone? What's he doing?"

Neil shook his head. "It's not as if he can spare the time to go wandering off 'getting his head together,' as Mr. Harman put it. Max knows they're behind with the shooting."

"You don't really think he went back to England?" said Emily.

"Of course not!" Neil was scornful. "He wouldn't just run off like that without telling us. Anyway, he knows that the sooner he finishes here, the sooner he can go home." He looked down at Stripes and patted him. "Max wouldn't leave us, would he, boy?"

Stripes seemed to know that something was wrong.

He sat down and looked at Neil solemnly, his head to one side.

"I suppose not," Emily said. "But where is he, then?"

"Dunno," Neil said. "Maybe Wanda's got ahold of him. Maybe she's witched him away somewhere."

"Should we take a look around the place?" Emily suggested.

Neil nodded. "Let's see what we can find. Maybe he's outside on the grounds."

"Maybe he's just . . . just fallen asleep or something," Emily suggested. She sighed. "It's more time being wasted, isn't it?"

Neil nodded. "I know what you're thinking — no Disneyland."

"Exactly," Emily said.

"So let's go," said Neil, and Stripes leaped up to go with them, wagging his tail and tugging on the leash.

An hour later, though, they hadn't found a single clue to Max's whereabouts. Because of the tight security, many parts of the studios were out of bounds, so their search was fairly limited. They looked everywhere in West Five and all around the grassy area where Stripes was usually exercised. They even went to talk to the men at the gates to see if they remembered Max going out — but no luck.

As they sat outside on the grass to think, Neil reached into the back pocket of his jeans and pulled out a small bone.

Emily looked at it in mock disgust. "You're the only person I know who keeps a bone in his pocket."

"You never know when a nice rib bone is going to come in handy," Neil said, grinning. He gave it to Stripes, who held it between his paws, ready for a good gnaw. "Em, if you stay out here with Stripes, I'll go and have a look around the dining hall."

"Get me something to eat, please. But you're not going to find Max in there now, are you?" asked Emily.

"'Course I'm not. I just thought I'd ask if anyone remembers seeing him this morning."

There was no sign of Max or Sue-Ellen in the dining hall. Neil ordered two burgers to go with a side order of french fries.

The woman serving remembered Max very well. "Such a polite boy," she said. "And what a lovely accent he has. Like all you Brits," she added with a smile.

"You remember him coming in this morning, then?" asked Neil.

The woman nodded. "Of course. It was seven o'clock and I'd just come on my shift. It's not everyone who wants a king-sized burger first thing in the morning!"

"Is that all he had?"

The woman thought for a few moments. "No, he

had hash browns and corn fritters and a side of French toast."

"And did he sit with anyone while he was eating?"

The woman handed over two brown paper bags containing Neil's burgers and fries. "No," she said. "He was by himself — and he was reading a comic book propped up on a sauce bottle in front of him. After he'd eaten, he had some water from the fountain and then he went out. I can remember it all because, as I said, I'd only just started work and there was hardly anyone in here."

"And you're sure he didn't talk to anyone? He didn't meet anyone and leave with them?" Neil asked.

The woman shook her head. "No one." She pointed toward the far door. "He finished his drink and then he went out that way. I knew he was in *Spook Spotting,* so I just thought he was going back to the set. You say he's disappeared?"

"For the moment he has," Neil said. "But I'm sure it'll be OK. I'm sure he'll come back." He hesitated. "Did he seem worried at all?"

"I couldn't say," the woman said.

Neil thanked her, then went back to Emily. "He was there, all right," he said. "And he seemed perfectly normal. He ate a huge breakfast."

Emily, who'd been stretched out in the sun with Stripes by her side, sat up and reached for her burger. "Thanks for this. But what does that prove?" she said, frowning.

"Nothing much." Neil shrugged. "Except, if he was going to run off somewhere — back to England, say — he'd hardly hang around to have a huge meal cooked first, would he?"

"No," Emily said. "So that means he's probably still here in the studios."

"Unless he's gone into town," suggested Neil.

"But why would he do that? And, anyway, he'd need somebody to drive him. No, he's got to be here, Neil. But where?"

"That's *exactly* what we've got to find out."

CHAPTER EIGHT

"**A**ny luck?" Sue-Ellen asked anxiously as Neil and Emily arrived back on the set.

Neil shook his head. "All we found out was that Max ate a big breakfast. The woman in the dining hall remembered serving him."

Sue-Ellen managed a smile. "At least we know he's not hungry, then." She crouched down to pat Stripes. "I was just about to come looking for you guys, actually. Mr. Harman wants to start on the next scene with Stripes and . . . well, it looks like he's going to use Abner in the part."

"So what will happen if Max doesn't come back today?" Emily asked.

Sue-Ellen sighed. "I really don't know. I guess the

police will have to be called in. And I'll have to file a missing persons report."

A look of horror crossed Emily's face. "It'll be really serious then."

"I know," Sue-Ellen said. "But let's hope it doesn't come to that. I'm convinced the answer to his disappearance is quite simple." She paused. "If only we knew what it was."

Neil glanced over at the spot where the cameras had been set up. Mr. Harman was giving instructions to Abner, who was wearing the navy blue T-shirt and the striped baseball cap that Max usually wore. "He didn't take long to get into Max's shoes, did he?" Neil commented.

Sue-Ellen made a face. "No, he didn't."

Neil handed Stripes's leash to Sue-Ellen and bent down to scratch the dog's nose. "Do well," he said, and then he added under his breath, "but not too well. Not with Abner."

The scene was a short one. Abner had to walk on his own along a deserted road. As Abner reached a tree, Stripes, much to the boy's surprise, was supposed to trot out and join him. Boy and dog would then walk down the road together.

Abner wouldn't even start filming until he'd called the makeup girl over to put more powder on his nose, which he said was shiny. He also asked to have some whitening gel put on his teeth.

Thelma turned to beam at everyone on the set. "That's my boy!" she said. "Such a professional. Likes to look perfect at all times."

Emily nudged Neil. "I thought he was just standing in for Max," she said. "Why is he bothering with all that?"

"Because he's a true professional," Neil whispered in Thelma's drawl, and Emily giggled.

The two of them watched as the scene took shape. Abner walked down the road and Stripes came out from behind a tree, then Abner bent down and petted him. Unfortunately, Stripes didn't seem to like Abner petting him and lay flat on the ground, cringing, as he was patted.

"It seems this dog is a bit nervous around you," Mr. Harman said, calling for the scene to be shot again. "And try to look as if you like the pooch. There's no dialogue in this scene, so you must show by your face and actions that you're not only surprised but *thrilled* to see Stripes. He's your best pal — your buddy!"

"Sure he is," Abner cried falsely. He knelt on the floor and put his face level with Stripes. "You're a great ole doggy, aren't you, boy? You're the greatest dog in the world!"

Neil gave Emily a look. He knew when people didn't really like dogs, and he'd never heard anything quite as fake as the way Abner was praising Stripes now.

After several more tries, the scene was actually

filmed. Thelma immediately burst into applause. "That was lovely, darling!" she cried to Abner. She appealed to Wanda, who was standing by, ready for the next scene. "Wasn't my boy great? What did you think, Wanda?"

"He was just fine," Wanda said. She shot a malicious glance toward Neil and Emily. "Seems we don't need Max here at all."

"That's enough, Wanda," Mr. Harman said.

All through the filming, Neil, Emily, and Sue-Ellen kept looking for Max. Neil was sure that he would walk up at any moment with a good reason for his disappearance.

But he didn't.

The scene was shot twice more from different angles and then Mr. Harman called a halt. "We may be able to use this scene and incorporate it into the film," he said. "Max and Abner are about the same height and build, so if we use the distant shots no one will know that it's not actually Max."

"Great idea!" Thelma said. She smiled at Neil and Emily. "I mean, it will help Max, too, won't it? When he gets back from wherever he's been he won't have quite as much work to do."

Mr. Harman glanced at his watch, then looked at Sue-Ellen. "I hope he turns up soon, this boy of yours," he said. "We're losing valuable camera time. Does anyone have any idea how much per minute I'm paying for the use of these studios?"

No one spoke except Wanda, who muttered, "You should have used homegrown talent from the beginning."

Thelma stepped forward. "I have an idea," she said. "I mean, just tell me if you think it's too ridiculous. . . ."

"No, let's have it," Mr. Harman said, while Neil leaned forward to make sure he didn't miss anything.

"It's just that if our friend Max has disappeared for a while — if he doesn't return for the rest of the day, for example, then maybe you should rethink *Spook Spotting*."

"In what way?" Mr. Harman asked.

"Well, maybe it should be reshot with Abner taking the lead role."

"Oh, Mom!" Abner cried, trying to look surprised and modest at the same time.

"I mean, Abner knows Max's part forward and backward. He could do all the scenes without any trouble. And then when Max comes back from wherever he went, he could play the minor role — the one Abner's got at the moment."

"She has it all worked out!" Emily hissed to Neil.

"And suppose Max doesn't come back?" Mr. Harman asked.

"Well . . ." Thelma looked around. "Maybe we could find some other kid to play the smaller part. It hardly needs someone of Abner's talent to do it." Her eyes lit upon Neil. "Like Max's young friend, for instance. Why couldn't Neil do it? You wanted a Brit in the film, after all."

Neil and Emily both gasped.

But Mr. Harman was shaking his head. "If I needed one, Thelma, I could get any of a dozen young actors with experience."

Sue-Ellen stepped forward. "I think we're all being a bit premature here," she said. "Max has only been missing for a few hours. He'll probably reappear at any moment and then things can carry on as normal."

"You're right," Mr. Harman said. "I suggest we continue on with the next scene and then all have a stroll around the place before lunch. Everyone should go to a different area and ask if anyone has seen Max. I'll go to the West Six studio and look there." He consulted his clipboard. "Wanda! Are you ready?" he called.

Wanda was bent over something in the corner and didn't seem to have heard him.

"Wanda!" Mr. Harman called. "You don't have that dog on the set with you again, do you?"

"I do," Wanda said. "Poor little Blossom gets lonely in the dressing room on her own, don't you, my precious?"

"Give me strength," Neil heard Mr. Harman mutter. The director cleared his throat. "Could she go back there, please, Wanda? I want some clear, fo-

cused acting from you. I don't get that if you're distracted by having your dog on the set."

"Dressing rooms are dangerous places," Wanda said. "Things disappear and people disappear. It is possible that a dog might disappear."

"At the moment, I would *really* like a dog to disappear from this set," Mr. Harman said in a level voice. He beckoned to Neil. "Please take it away, Neil."

"She has a name!" Wanda put in.

"Please take Blossom back to Wanda's dressing room, Neil. And then, if you wouldn't mind, could you stay there and dog-sit for half an hour or so — just until we've shot this scene?"

"I'd be happy to," Neil said. He really liked the tiny Chihuahua and was sure she enjoyed being treated like a dog rather than a toy.

Wanda narrowed her eyes at Neil as she handed him the key to her dressing room. "And I'm warning you, I know exactly what's in that room, boy."

Neil pretended not to hear her. "You stay here," he said to Emily. "Come tell me as soon as Max turns up."

Emily nodded. "*If* he turns up . . ." she said in a small, worried voice.

CHAPTER NINE

"**T**here's still no sign of him anywhere!" Emily wailed.

"Not a clue," Neil said glumly.

It was nearly two o'clock in the afternoon and everyone was back on the set of *Spook Spotting*. They'd had lunch in the dining hall and searched everywhere for Max. Now Mr. Harman had called a meeting on the set to see if anyone had any ideas.

"I'll have to call his mom in England if he doesn't turn up soon," Sue-Ellen said. "I'm just dreading doing that."

"She'll be so worried," Emily said.

"But on the other hand, she may know something," put in Mr. Harman. "Maybe Max called to tell her what he's up to."

"I think we should let him come back of his own accord," Thelma said. "As Mr. Harman said earlier, maybe it's all a little too much for him and he needs time to get his head together. Perhaps he had to go home — back to England — to do that." She glanced fondly at Abner. "If he has, then my boy will have to step in and save the film."

"Max got caught with my Blossom's things and now he's sulking somewhere," Wanda declared. "He wants us all to worry about him and then he'll just come back and expect everyone to fuss over him."

"Max isn't at all like that!" Neil said heatedly. "He hates people making a fuss over him."

"Well, you would say that, wouldn't you?" Wanda said.

Neil opened his mouth to say more but was stopped by Sue-Ellen shaking her head at him.

Mr. Harman swept a hand wearily across his brow. "OK, Max has been missing for nearly seven hours now and it's time to get serious. Does anyone have anything to add — anything sensible to add — before I make the decision to call the police?"

Everyone looked solemn and said nothing.

"This is not an easy decision. Having police everywhere is going to make it very difficult to continue filming *Spook Spotting*. In fact, it may become impossible."

"But my boy could —" Thelma began, but she stopped immediately when Mr. Harman glared at her.

"What do you think the police will do?" one of the cameramen asked.

"To start with, bring in police dogs and search the place methodically," Mr. Harman said.

Neil suddenly clapped a hand to his head. "Hey!" he shouted, and everyone looked at him. "That's given me an idea, Mr. Harman. *Police dogs.*" He pointed to Stripes. "Why didn't I think of it before? I must be crazy."

Sue-Ellen looked gratefully at Neil. "Of course!"

"What are you talking about?" Mr. Harman asked, frowning.

"Well, we haven't actually asked Stripes to find Max, have we?" Sue-Ellen said. "That's what you're thinking, isn't it, Neil?"

Neil nodded eagerly.

"But the dog's been with you when you've been looking," Mr. Harman said.

"Yes, he has," agreed Neil. "But we haven't actually given him something of Max's and told him to find Max.

"My dog's smart but he's not psychic," Sue-Ellen said. "If no one's actually told him that Max is missing, how could he be expected to know?"

"And you think that if you tell him to find Max now, he will?" said Mr. Harman, sounding doubtful.

"He might," Sue-Ellen said.

"No acting dog is going to find a missing person,"

Wanda put in scornfully. "Dogs have to be specially trained to do stuff like that."

"But it's worth a try," Emily said.

"OK," said Mr. Harman. "I'm not sure that I believe it's possible, but I guess it is worth a try." He looked at Neil. "Have you got something of Max's?"

Neil thought. Several of the things Max wore in the film had been worn by Abner since and would have his scent on them, too. "I'll go look in his dressing room," he said.

"Just be quick, kid," said Mr. Harman.

Neil was about to run off when Stripes, who was by his side, suddenly started growling. He lowered his body to the floor and made a low, rumbling noise in the back of his throat.

"What's wrong with him?" Wanda said, and then she added, "He's gone completely crazy, by the look of it."

Neil looked at the dog, rather alarmed. "The last two times he behaved like that," he said, "there was an earthquake."

"Off you go, kid," ordered Mr. Harman.

But Neil didn't move. He watched Stripes pick himself up from the floor and give a small yelp. Then the dog trotted toward the door, went back to Neil, and repeated the action all over again.

"What's he doing now?" Thelma asked. "I've never seen a dog act so crazy in all my life."

"I think he wants us to get out of the studio," Neil said.

"Why should we do that?" someone asked.

"Well, it might be an earthquake," Neil said uncertainly. He knew that Stripes was smart enough to detect earthquakes, but it wasn't going to be easy to persuade a whole crowd of people to believe that, too.

"Well, I'm not rushing all over the place just because of a crazy dog!" Thelma said.

"Neither am I," declared Wanda.

Mr. Harman scratched his head anxiously and stared at Stripes, who continued to run back and forth between Neil and the door, all the time giving little yelps.

"I'm going with Stripes, and so is Emily," Neil said, making up his mind.

"And so am I," declared Sue-Ellen. "I know that dog of mine, and he never does anything without a reason."

"Well, I'm staying here," Abner said. "It's bad enough having the film disrupted without following that crazy mutt."

"I don't know. . . ." Mr. Harman said doubtfully, watching Stripes. "He's usually a pretty smart dog."

"We've had two quakes already this week," Sue-Ellen said. "I think we should go."

"Oh, come *on*. Don't waste any more time," Neil said, dragging Emily along. "You're all crazy if you don't come outside right *now*."

Mr. Harman suddenly made up his mind. "OK," he shouted. "West Five studio is being evacuated. Everyone — and I mean everyone — is to leave *immediately*!"

There was a rush toward the big double doors at the end of the studio, which led out to a patch of gravel. Within just a few seconds, everyone was outside. Mr. Harman began ushering them all toward the grassy area some distance away from the building. Once there, one of the cameramen put his head flat to the ground to listen. "There's a rumble. There's one coming for sure!"

Wanda suddenly gave a high-pitched scream. "Blossom! Oh, my poor Blossom is in my dressing room! Oh, save her, someone!"

Neil stared at Wanda and then, before he could stop and think about whether it was a smart thing to do, he turned and ran across the grass, plunged back through the double doors, and raced across the deserted studio floor. As he kicked open the fire door that led to the dressing rooms and ran along the corridor, he was aware that Stripes was running, too, zipping around the corner and scrabbling at the door of Wanda's dressing room as Neil fumbled with the key.

"Blossom!" Neil shouted. As he wrenched the door open, Blossom leaped out of her basket and charged across the floor. "Come on!" Neil panted. "Let's go!"

Neil and Stripes ran back, faster and faster, neck

and neck, as if their lives depended on it. Suddenly, Neil realized that fat little Blossom couldn't keep up. Wanda had pampered her so much that she just couldn't run. Turning around, he raced back up the corridor to where the terrified dog lay gasping on the floor. He scooped her up and then he and Stripes ran through the studio, shot through the open doors, and raced across the gravel, arriving back at the grassy area in barely a minute and a half from Wanda's first cry.

Wanda shrieked with joy and fell upon the little dog, who was panting in Neil's arms.

"Your dog nearly didn't make it out of there!" Neil

exploded. "She couldn't run. We had to go back for her, all because you don't care for her correctly."

Wanda looked sheepish, but she said nothing as she turned away, burying her face in Blossom's coat.

Mr. Harman was running around, shouting instructions. As Neil flopped down, panting, beside Emily, there came the high-pitched screeching of a fire alarm and a loudspeaker announcement saying that everyone must leave the studios.

The earth began to shake almost immediately. Emily clutched Neil and closed her eyes while the whole world seemed to shudder and tip as though it would never stop, and a deep thundering came from beneath the ground.

"Oh!" Neil gasped, but he hardly had time to be frightened as he stared in amazement at the West Five studio. There was a deafening creaking sound and a huge crack appeared down the front of the studio building. For a second nothing happened and then one half of the building came crashing down with a mighty roar.

"I don't believe it. . . ." Neil said in a shocked voice.

"Oh, Neil! How awful!" Emily cried.

The ground continued to shake and the shattered building shifted again. A cloud of dust and smoke rose into the air. Several planks of wood clattered to the ground, and there was a tinkle of broken glass.

As quickly as it had started, everything became still. For a few moments, no one said anything. Everyone stood like statues, hardly daring to breathe. Eventually, Mr. Harman spoke. "I think that's it, folks. I've counted to fifty and we don't seem to be getting any aftershocks. I think it's safe to say that it's over."

Everyone's eyes went to the heap of broken wood and stone that, a moment before, had been their studio.

"We all got out and I don't think anyone's hurt — that's the main thing," Mr. Harman went on. He gave a rather bitter laugh. "It's just unfortunate that it's the West Five studio that seems to have taken the brunt of it." He gestured toward the rest of the complex. "No one else seems to have been affected much."

"We got out just in time," Neil said hoarsely. He reached for Stripes and hugged him. "You fantastic dog! You deserve a medal."

"He sure does," agreed Mr. Harman.

Emily let out a cry.

"It's OK, Em," Neil comforted her. "It's all right. We're all safe."

"Max isn't!" Emily said. "He might be somewhere inside the studio. He might be lying trapped and seriously injured. You've all forgotten that, haven't you?"

CHAPTER TEN

Sue-Ellen gasped. "Emily's right!" she cried out. "We're all so busy worrying about ourselves that we've forgotten about Max. What if he's still in there?"

"That kid!" Mr. Harman said, and Neil heard him mutter something under his breath.

He shook his head. "We've searched all of West Five, though. He *can't* be anywhere inside."

"He might be. . . ." Emily said in a worried voice.

"If he is, he must be invisible," one of the cameramen said. "We've looked everywhere."

"He's caused us nothing but trouble," Wanda complained. She had Blossom in her arms but seemed to be considering whether or not to put her on the ground. Finally, she did so, and the little dog ran around and around her feet, barking excitedly.

Beyond the studios, the blaring sirens of fire engines could be heard coming along the freeway. People were running up from the other buildings and staring in consternation at the West Five studio, while Mr. Harman was reassuring them that everyone had gotten out all right and no one was hurt.

"Someone has to go look for Max," Emily persisted.

Sue-Ellen rubbed her face with her hand. "The firemen will do that," she said. "They've got special heat-seeking cameras."

"Yes, the police and firemen will make a thorough search for him," Thelma put in. Neil noticed that she'd gone very pale and her voice sounded shaky. "I'm sure he'll . . . he'll be OK."

"Thelma seems really upset and worried about Max," he whispered to Emily. "Maybe we've got her all wrong."

"Maybe," Emily said. She turned to Neil. "Why can't we still use Stripes to look for Max?" she asked urgently.

Neil shrugged. "I suppose we could. . . ."

"I guess we'd better wait until the police come and do the job properly," Sue-Ellen said. "It might be dangerous in there."

"I can't bear to wait that long," Emily cried. "Can't we start looking for him now?"

"Yes, can't we?" Neil asked, putting his hand on

Stripes. "If he's in the studio somewhere, I bet Stripes can find him."

"I really don't think you should go into the building," Sue-Ellen said. "It needs to be checked out first for safety purposes." She glanced at Neil's disappointed face. "Look, OK, I'll have a word with Mr. Harman and see what he thinks."

Sue-Ellen went over to the director and started talking with him. As Neil waited, he noticed that Thelma was acting rather oddly. At first, she was deep in hushed conversation with Abner, then she glanced around at Emily and Neil a couple of times.

Before Neil could draw his sister's attention to Thelma, Sue-Ellen hurried back to them.

"Mr. Harman says we'll have to wait," she said. "There are all kinds of formalities to go through before anyone's allowed back in the building."

Neil sighed impatiently.

"What will happen now about the film?" Emily asked. "How can they carry on without a studio?"

Sue-Ellen shrugged. "Maybe we can use another one. It depends whether they're all booked up." She glanced down at Stripes. "I'm going to get Stripes some water from the dining hall," she said, handing the dog's leash to Neil. "Are you two sure you're OK?"

Neil and Emily nodded. As Sue-Ellen disappeared toward the dining hall, Emily whispered in Neil's ear, "Don't wait for the firemen. Can't you take Stripes and go search now?"

Neil nodded. "I've already decided to," he said. "I'd better not go in the wrecked part though. I'll just look around the place and see if I can find anything." He sighed. "I haven't been able to get anything personal of Max's, though, have I? Nothing for Stripes to sniff."

Emily suddenly beamed at him. "I just remembered! I have a postcard of Max's in my pocket. He gave it to me last night and asked me to mail it for him."

"I don't know if it'll have his scent on it. . . ." Neil began, but as Emily's face fell he took the postcard from her. "We'll give it a try, though."

Emily handed the rather battered postcard to Neil, who sat down on the grass so that his face was level with Stripes's. He put the postcard right under

Stripes's nose. "Listen, boy," he said. "Max is missing and we want you to find him."

The dog looked at Neil intelligently, his ears pricked.

"Find Max!" Neil repeated.

Stripes sniffed at the card, then stood up, tail wagging.

"I think he understands!" Emily said. She looked around to make sure no one was watching them. "I'm coming with you!"

Neil shook his head. "Better not. We don't want us *both* to get in trouble."

"Be careful, then!" Emily said.

Neil grinned encouragingly at his sister and set off, with Stripes walking close behind him.

"OK, boy. Find Max," Neil said under his breath. They walked around the crumbled side of the West Five studio and continued across a graveled area toward some shabby-looking buildings. "You saved Blossom, you saved us from the earthquake, now you've got to find Max," Neil went on. "I know you can!"

The dog looked up at Neil and, from his brown eyes, it seemed he understood.

Stripes stopped outside the first building they came to, which had heavy, padlocked double doors and was as large as an aircraft hangar. As he sniffed underneath the doors and scrabbled in the gravel, Neil began to feel quite excited. Suddenly, Stripes tugged at the leash and moved off, still keeping his nose to the ground.

"Not the right place, huh?" Neil said.

Behind them, the fire engines had drawn up on the gravel outside the West Five studio and, just as a precaution, the firefighters were uncoiling the long rubber water hoses. At any other time, Neil would have enjoyed the excitement of the earthquake, but now he had other things on his mind.

The next building he and Stripes arrived at was an old film property storehouse. Max had told them that it was used to store painted backdrops and fake house fronts from earlier productions at the studios.

Stripes stopped outside one of the green painted doors and turned around in a circle, sniffing the air.

Neil couldn't help laughing. "What are you doing, boy?" he said. "We're looking for Max, remember? Find Max!"

Once again, Stripes shot off, pulling Neil with him — but instead of going along to the next building he went around to the back of the props storehouse, sniffed eagerly at the ground, and then began digging at the earth in front of a door.

"Is something buried there, or are you trying to burrow under it?" Neil asked him.

Stripes continued to dig with his front paws and Neil noticed that there was a heavy key in the lock of the door. He pulled at the handle and the door opened.

"Unlocked," Neil murmured to himself. "That's strange. It's lucky that nothing around here's been damaged by the earthquake." He looked down at Stripes. "Is this where you want us to go?" he asked, and the dog gave a short, low bark.

"I'll take that as a yes," said Neil.

Feeling his heart thudding with excitement, Neil went through the door. He found himself in a long, dark, high-ceilinged corridor with a row of doors leading off it.

"Where do we go from here?" Neil asked Stripes quietly. "Which door?"

Stripes looked at him, his head to one side. Then he put his nose down to the ground and began to sniff his way along the corridor. At the sixth door, he stopped and looked up at Neil. He gave another bark.

"This one? Here?" Neil asked.

But Stripes was already up on his hind legs, pushing at the door. It opened into a vast warehouse stacked with tall pieces of painted canvas scenery. The only light came from grimy skylights in the ceiling. Neil looked up at the painted scenes and saw that they were a backdrop for an ancient Egyptian tomb, with hieroglyphics and wall paintings showing ancient kings and queens. A little farther along, he came to some more props — mummy cases and all kinds of gold-painted pots and boxes, and a large square box containing a replica of an Egyptian coffin, surrounded by statues of animal-headed gods and goddesses.

"This is spooky!" Neil whispered under his breath. It felt odd to be in this silent, creepy place surrounded by all the props and scenery from long-ago films.

Stripes gave a sudden whine. He looked up at Neil and sniffed the air.

Neil shook his head. "Max can't be around here, Stripes. What would he be doing in the middle of all this stuff?"

Stripes whined again, then he bounded away from Neil, pulling the leash out of his hand. He dashed toward a mummy case that was standing in a corner and leaped up at it, barking.

"What's up?" Neil said urgently. "What is it?"

Stripes continued to bark as Neil approached the case. It was made of papier mâché and embossed in brilliant blues and golds, with the face and body of a young Egyptian king painted on it, his crossed arms holding a rod and a staff.

Nervously, Neil put his hand out toward the case. It moved, and a strange voice came from behind the painted mask. Neil gasped and jumped backward. But Stripes leaped at the mummy case, whining excitedly, and the muffled voice suddenly sounded familiar to Neil.

"Max?" he cried, frantically opening the case.

Inside was a scared-looking Max, with his hands and feet tied.

Neil pulled frantically at the ropes. "What are you doing here?" he exclaimed. "Are you all right? No one could find you — they thought you'd gone home. And there's been an earthquake!"

Max took a deep breath. "At last! What kept you? And yeah — I felt the earthquake. Is anyone hurt?" he said in a rush.

Neil shook his head. "West Five studio is a bit of a mess, though." He grinned. "We looked everywhere, but it was Stripes who found you." Both boys looked down at the dog. He was sitting loyally beside Max and looking up at them as if to say he knew he'd done a good job.

"You won't believe how I ended up here," Max began. He stopped as Stripes turned to stare into a shadowy corner, growling menacingly.

"What now?" Neil asked in a low voice.

There was a brightly painted screen standing in the corner, and, all at once, Stripes leaped behind it. There was a short shriek, a scuffle, and a lot of barking from Stripes. The screen fell over and Thelma stood there, cowering away from Stripes, who was looking very fierce.

"Thelma!" Neil exclaimed, astonished. What on earth was going on here?

"I was just going to tell you — it was her," Max said. "She tied me up and put me in the mummy case."

"*What?*" said Neil, unable to believe his ears.

Thelma tried to step forward but was prevented from doing so by Stripes darting toward her ankles, growling.

"What did you do that for?" Neil asked Thelma.

Her voice shook. "It was just a spur of the moment thing," she said weakly.

"But you must have known someone would find Max before too long," Neil pointed out.

"I only needed him out of the way for a while," Thelma said sullenly. There was no sign of the wide plastic smile now.

"But *why?*" Neil asked while Max rubbed at his numb hands, trying to get some feeling back into them. "You might as well tell us."

Thelma shook her head, then she seemed to realize that she had been truly found out. "I wanted

Max's part for Abner," she said dully. "I thought if Max was missing for a day, then Mr. Harman might lose his patience and give my boy his part. I told Max that you wanted to meet him here. Then I grabbed him, tied him up, and pushed him into the mummy case."

"Yeah. Thanks a heap," Max said, kicking at the ropes that had bound him.

"And I suppose it was you who took Blossom's things as well?" Neil demanded.

Thelma stared at the floor, looking very embarrassed. "It was. I wanted to cause trouble on the set."

"Oh, you did, did you?" came a new voice.

Stripes gave a joyful bark as Sue-Ellen appeared from behind a scaled-down replica of a pyramid. She ran over to Max. "I knew you wouldn't have gone home," she said, giving him a hug. "And I heard everything you said, Thelma. You're very lucky Max is all right. You could have suffocated him in that mummy case, and then the police would have been involved as well. In fact, you're lucky that I don't call them right now."

Thelma looked ashamed. "It was just to help Abner," she protested. "He would have been wonderful in that part. And then when we had the earthquake I realized what a terrible thing I'd done. I ran over here as quickly as I could to see if Max was all right."

"And he was, no thanks to you," Sue-Ellen said dryly.

Neil was looking at Sue-Ellen in astonishment. "But how did you find us?"

"I followed you, of course," she said. "I was on my way back from the dining hall when I saw you running off with Stripes and I realized what you were up to. I knew I wouldn't be able to stop you, but I was worried about both of you."

Max, free at last, knelt on the ground. "Stripes!" he called. "Come here, boy."

Stripes trotted over to Max and he flung his arms around the dog — probably for the first time ever, Neil realized, grinning.

"Thanks for finding me," Max said, burying his face in Stripes's fur. "You're one dog in a million!"

Sue-Ellen and Neil smiled at each other, both of them immensely relieved.

Neil knew that Max had bonded with Stripes at

last, and from that moment on, they'd always have that special "invisible rope" that Sue-Ellen had talked about.

"So the filming's all back on schedule now," Neil said two mornings later.

"Unbelievably, yes," said Sue-Ellen. "It was just so lucky that Mr. Harman was able to rent another studio right away."

"And *extra* lucky Max and Stripes were able to make up for lost time," Neil pointed out.

Neil, Emily, and Max were sitting on stools at the breakfast bar in Sue-Ellen's apartment, where she was making French toast. Stripes was sitting with his head on Max's foot, and every time Max took a bite of French toast, he dropped a piece into Stripes's open mouth. The two of them were best friends now.

Sue-Ellen smiled fondly at them both. "I should stop you from doing that, Max, but I won't. It's just so good to see you getting along so well together. And it's made such a difference to the film. Every scene works beautifully now."

"Even Abner's almost bearable now that Thelma's been banned from the set," Emily added as she, Neil, and Max made goofy, smiling, Thelma-like faces at one another.

Sue-Ellen nodded. "I feel a little sorry for the poor kid, actually. It's not his fault he's got such a pushy mom."

"More amazingly, though," put in Max, "I actually saw Wanda taking Blossom for a walk yesterday! They were wearing matching jackets, but at least it's a start."

"So really, the film's ahead of schedule," Neil began casually.

"Not ahead. Just about OK," Sue-Ellen said. The corners of her mouth were twitching slightly.

"So, do you think it might be possible —" Neil went on.

"— to go to Disneyland?" Emily finished in an impatient rush. "Oh, please!"

Sue-Ellen laughed. "I was keeping it a secret, but as a matter of fact there's a car coming for us in exactly one hour. We're spending the whole day in Disneyland and going back to Mr. Harman's house later for a barbecue."

There was a shout of joy from everyone, and a bark from Stripes.

"Fantastic," said Neil. He smiled at the others. "What a vacation this has turned out to be!"